In The Blue Pike

Volume 2

by

Georg Ebers

Double9 BOOKS

In The Blue Pike
Volume 2
by Georg Ebers

ISBN: 978-93-76392-32-2

Published by

DOUBLE 9 BOOKS

2/13-B, Ansari Road
Daryaganj, New Delhi – 110002
info@double9books.com
www.double9books.com
Tel. 011-40042856

ABOUT THE AUTHOR

Georg Moritz Ebers (1837–1898) was a prominent German Egyptologist and novelist, widely recognized for his contributions to the study of ancient Egypt. He is particularly renowned for acquiring the Ebers Papyrus in 1872, a key medical text from ancient Egypt that contains valuable knowledge about the medical practices of the time. This papyrus is one of the oldest surviving medical documents in the world and helped cement Ebers' reputation in the field of Egyptology. Ebers was born in Berlin, Germany, and he pursued a career that spanned both scholarly and literary pursuits. He studied medicine, and his interests in ancient civilizations led him to Egyptology, where he made lasting contributions. In addition to his scholarly work, Ebers was also a prolific writer, publishing historical novels that often explored ancient Egypt. His literary works were quite popular during his lifetime, and he became one of the leading voices in promoting the study of ancient Egypt. In addition to his achievements in Egyptology, Ebers helped raise awareness about the importance of preserving ancient Egyptian culture and contributed to academic discussions on the ancient world.

CONTENTS

CHAPTER IV....7
CHAPTER V....17
CHAPTER VI....27
CHAPTER VII....33

CHAPTER IV

The ropedancer, Kuni, really had been with the sick mother and her babes, and had toiled for them with the utmost diligence.

The unfortunate woman was in great distress.

The man who had promised to take her in his cart to her native village of Schweinfurt barely supported himself and his family by the tricks of his trained poodles. He made them perform their very best feats in the taverns, under the village lindens, and at the fairs. But the children who gazed at the four-footed artists, though they never failed to give hearty applause, frequently paid in no other coin. He would gladly have helped the unfortunate woman, but to maintain the wretched mother and her twins imposed too heavy a burden upon the kind-hearted vagabond, and he had withdrawn his aid.

Then the ropedancer met her. True, she herself was in danger of being left lying by the wayside; but she was alone, and the mother had her children. These were two budding hopes, while she had nothing more to expect save the end—the sooner the better. There could be no new happiness for her.

And yet, to have found some one who was even more needy than she, lifted her out of herself, and to have power to be and do something in her behalf pleased her, nay, even roused an emotion akin to that which, in better days, she had felt over a piece of good fortune which others envied. Perhaps she herself might be destined to die on the highway, without consolation, the very next day; but she could save this unhappy woman from it, and render her end easier. Oh, how rich Lienhard's gold coins made her! Yet if, instead of three, there had been as many dozens, she would have placed the larger portion in the twins' pillows. How it must soothe their mother's heart! Each one was a defence against hunger and want. Besides, the gold had been fairly burning her hand. It came from Lienhard. Had it not been for Cyriax and the crowd of people in the room, she would have made him take it back—she alone knew why.

How did this happen?

Why did every fibre of her being rebel against receiving even the smallest trifle from the man to whom she would gladly have given the whole world? Why, after she had summoned up courage and approached

Lienhard to restore his gift, had she felt such keen resentment and bitter suffering when the landlord of The Blue Pike stopped her?

As she now seized his gold, it seemed as though she saw Lienhard before her. She had already told Cyriax how she met the aristocratic Nuremberg patrician, a member of the ancient and noble Groland family, whom his native city had now made an ambassador so young. But what secretly bound her to him had never passed her lips.

Once in her life she had felt something which placed her upon an equal footing with the best and purest of her sex—a great love for one from whom she asked nothing, nothing at all, save to be permitted to think of him and to sacrifice everything, everything for him—even life. So strange had been the course of this love, that people would have doubted her sanity or her truthfulness had she described it to them.

While standing before St. Sebald's church in Nuremberg, the vision of the young Councillor's bride at first made a far stronger impression upon her mind than his own. Then her gaze rested on Lienhard. As he had chosen the fairest of women, the bride had also selected the tallest, most stately, and certainly the best and wisest of men. During her imprisonment the image of this rare couple had been constantly before her. Not until, through the young husband's intercession, she had regained her liberty, after he prevented her kissing his hand and, to soothe her, had stroked her hair and cheeks in the magistrate's room, did the most ardent gratitude take possession of her soul. From this emotion, which filled heart and mind, a glowing wealth of other feelings had blossomed like buds upon a rosebush. Everything in her nature had attracted her toward him, and the desire to devote herself to him, body and soul, shed the last drop of blood in her heart for him, completely ruled her. His image rose before her day and night, sometimes alone, sometimes with his beautiful bride. Not only to him, but to her also she would joyfully have rendered the most menial service, merely to be near them and to be permitted to show that the desire to prove her gratitude had become the object of her life.

When, with good counsel for the future, he dismissed her from the chief magistrate's room, he had asked her where she was to be found in case he should have anything to say to her. It seemed as though, from mingled alarm and joy, her heart would stop beating. If her lodgings, instead of an insignificant tavern, had been her own palace, she would gladly have opened all its gates to him, yet a feverish thrill ran through her limbs at the thought that he might seek her among her vagabond companions, and ask in return for his kindness what he would never have presumed to seek had she been the child of reputable parents, yet which, with mingled anger and happiness, she resolved not to refuse.

During the day and the night when she expected his visit, she had become aware that she, who had never cared for any man save for the gifts he bestowed, was fired with love for Lienhard. Such ardent yearning could torture only a loving heart, yet what she felt was very unlike the love with which she was familiar in songs, and had seen in other girls; for she by no means thought with jealous rancour of the woman to whom he belonged, body and soul—his beautiful wife. It rather seemed to her that she was his, and he would no longer be the same if he were separated from her, nay, as if her very love was hers also. When she heard a noise outside of her little room she started, and eagerly as she yearned to see him, blissful as she thought it must be to sink upon his breast and offer him her lips to kiss, the bold ropedancer, who never cared for the opinions of others, could not shake off, even for a moment, the fear of wronging the fair wife who had a better right to him. Instead of hating her, or even wishing to share the heart of the man she loved with his bride, she shrank from the approaching necessity of clouding her young happiness as though it were the direst misfortune. Yet she felt that its prevention lay, not in her own hands, but in those of Fate. Should it please Destiny to lead Lienhard to her and inspire him with a desire for her love, all resistance, she knew, would be futile. So she began to repeat several paternosters that he might remain away from her. But her yearning was so great that she soon desisted, and again and again went to the window with a fervent wish that he might come.

In the terrible tumult of her heart she had forgotten to eat or to drink since early morning, and at last, in the afternoon, some one knocked at the door, and the landlady called her.

While she was hurriedly smoothing her thick black hair and straightening her best gown, which she had put on for him in the morning, she heard the hostess say that Herr Groland of the Council was waiting for her downstairs. Every drop of blood left her glowing cheeks, and the knees which never trembled on the rope shook as she descended the narrow steps.

He came forward to meet her in the entry, holding out his hand with open- hearted frankness. How handsome and how good he was! No one wore that look who desired aught which must be hidden under the veil of darkness. Ere her excited blood had time to cool, he had beckoned to her to follow him into the street, where a sedan chair was standing.

An elderly lady of dignified bearing looked out and met her eyes with a pleasant glance. It was Frau Sophia, the widow of Herr Conrad Schurstab of the Council, one of the richest and most aristocratic noblewomen in the city. Lienhard had told her about the charming prisoner who had been released and begged her to help him bring her back to a respectable and orderly life. The lady needed an assistant who, now that it was hard for her to stoop, would inspect the linen closets, manage the poultry yard- her pride—and keep an eye on the children when they came to visit their grandmother. So she instantly accompanied Lienhard to the tavern, and Kuni pleased her. But it would have been difficult not to feel some degree of sympathy for the charming young creature who, in great embarrassment, yet joyously as though released from a heavy burden, raised her large blue eyes to the kind stranger.

It was cold in the street, and as Kuni had come out without any wrap, Frau Schurstab, in her friendly consideration, shortened the, conference. Lienhard Uroland had helped her with a few words, and when the sedan chair and the young Councillor moved down the street all the necessary details were settled. The vagrant had bound herself and assumed duties, though they were very light ones. She was to move that evening into the distinguished widow's house, not as a servant, but as the old lady's assistant.

Loni, the manager of the company of rope-dancers, had watched the negotiations from the taproom. During their progress each of the three windows was filled with heads, but no one had been able to hear what was whispered in the street. Just as the curious spectators were hoping that now they might perhaps guess what the aristocratic lady wanted with Kuni, the sedan chair began to move, and the young girl entered the hot room to tell Loni that she would leave the company that day forever.

"In-de-e-ed?" Loni asked in astonishment, lifting the gold circlet which rested on his head. Then he passed his hand through the coal-black hair which, parted in the middle, fell in smooth strands upon his neck, and exerted all his powers of persuasion to convince her of the folly of her plan. After his arguments were exhausted he raised his voice louder. As usual, when excited by anger, he swung his lower right arm to and fro, feeling the prominent muscles with his left hand. But Kuni remained resolute, and when be at last perceived that his opposition only increased her obstinacy, he exclaimed:

"Then rush on to your destruction! The day will come when you will see where you belong. If only it doesn't arrive too late. A man grows twelve and a woman thirty-six months older every year."

With these words he turned his back upon her, and the clown brought the amount of wages which was due.

Many an eye grew dim with tears when Kuni bade farewell to her companions. Shortly after sunset she was welcomed to Frau Schurstab's house.

The first greeting was friendly, and she received nothing but kindness and indulgent treatment afterward. She had a sunny chamber of her own, and how large and soft her bed was! But while, when on the road with

Loni's band, if they could reach no town, she had often slept soundly and sweetly on a heap of straw, here she spent one restless night after another.

During the first a series of questions disturbed her slumber. Was it really only the desire to take her from her vagabond life which had induced Lienhard to open this house to her? Did he not perhaps also cherish the wish to keep her near him? He had certainly come to her with Frau Schurstab to protect her reputation. Had it not been so he might have left the matron at home; for Loni and everybody in the company knew that she never troubled herself about gossip. Last year she had obtained a leave of absence from Loni, who was making a tour of the little Frank towns, and spent the carnival season in revelry with a sergeant of the Nurembreg soldiers. When the booty he had gained in Italy was squandered, she gave him his dismissal. Her reputation among her companions was neither better nor worse than that of the other strolling players who, like her, were born on the highway, yet she was glad that Lienhard had tried to spare her. Or had he only come with the old noblewoman on account of his own fair name?

Perhaps—her pulses again throbbed faster at the thought—he had not ventured to come alone because some feeling for her stirred in his own heart, and, spite of his beautiful young wife, he did not feel safe from her. Then Fran Schurstab was to serve as a shield. This conjecture flattered her vanity and reconciled her to the step which she had taken and already began to regret.

But suppose he really felt no more for her than the forester who finds a child lost in the woods, and guides it into the right path? How would she endure that? Yet, were it otherwise, if he was like the rest of men, if he profited by what her whole manner must betray to him, how should she face his wife, who undoubtedly would soon come to call on her aunt?

All these questions roused a tumult of unprecedented violence in her young, ardent, inexperienced soul, which was renewed each successive night. It became more and more difficult for her to understand why she had left Loni's band and entered into relations for which she was not suited, and in which she could never, never be at ease or feel happy.

Nothing was lacking in this wealthy household, not even kindness and love. Frau Sophia was indulgent and friendly, even when Kuni, whose heart and brain were occupied with so many other thoughts, neglected or forgot anything. The matron's grandchildren, of whom she often had charge, soon became warmly attached to her. While among the rope-dancers she had been fond of children, and many a little one who journeyed with the band held out its arms to her more joyously than to its own mother. There was something in her nature that attracted them. Besides, her skilful hands could show them many a rare trick, and she could sing numerous songs new to the Schurstab boys and girls, which she had picked up here and there. Then, too, she permitted many a prank which no one else would have allowed. Her duties connected with the household linen and the poultry yard, its owner's pride, were so easily performed, that in her leisure hours she often voluntarily helped the housekeeper. At first the latter eyed her askance, but she soon won her affection. Both she and her mistress showed her as much attention as the gardener bestows upon a wild plant which he has transferred to good soil, where it thrives under his care.

She kept aloof from the servants, and neither man nor maid molested her. Perhaps this was due to foolish arrogance, for after they had learned from rumour that Kuni had danced on the tight rope, they considered themselves far superior. The younger maids timidly kept out of her way, and Kuni surpassed them in pride and looked down upon them, because her free artist blood rebelled against placing herself on the plane of a servitor. She did not vouchsafe them a word, yet neither did she allow any of them to render her even the most trivial service. But she could not escape Seifried, the equerry of her mistress's eldest son. At first, according to her custom, she had roused the handsome fellow's hopes by fiery glances which she could not restrain. Now he felt that she cared for him, and in his honest fashion offered to make her his beloved wife; but she refused his suit, at first kindly, then angrily. As he still persisted she begged the housekeeper, though she saw that matchmaking was her delight, to keep him away.

Even in March Frau Sophia thanked Lienhard for the new inmate of her household, who far exceeded her expectations. In April her praise became still warmer, only she regretted that Kuni's pretty face was losing its fresh colour and her well-formed figure its roundness. She was sorry, too, that she so often seemed lost in thought, and appeared less merry while playing with the children.

Lienhard and his young wife excused the girl's manner. Comfortable as she was now, she was still a prisoned bird. It would be unnatural, nay, suspicious, if she did not sometimes long for the old freedom and her former companions. She would also remember at times the applause of the multitude. The well-known Loni, her former employer, had besought him to win her back to his company, complaining loudly of her loss, because it was difficult to replace her with an equally skilful young artist. It was now evident how mistaken the juggler had been when he asserted that Kuni, who was born among vagrants, would never live in a respectable family. He, Lienhard, had great pleasure in knowing that the girl, on the road to ruin, had been saved by Frau Sophia's goodness.

Lienhard's father had died shortly after Kuni entered her new home. Every impulse to love dalliance, she felt, must shrink before this great sorrow. The idea sustained her hopes. She could not expect him to seek her again until the first bitterness of grief for the loss of this beloved relative had passed away. She could wait, and she succeeded in doing so patiently.

But week after week went by and there was no change in his conduct. Then a great anxiety overpowered her, and this did not escape his notice; for one day, while his young wife hung on his arm and added a few brief words of sympathy, he asked Kuni if she was ill or if she needed anything; but she answered curtly in the negative and hurried into the garden, where the children, with merry shouts, were helping the gardener to free the beds of crocuses and budding tulips from the pine boughs which had protected them from the frosts of winter.

Another sleepless night followed this incident. It was useless to deceive herself. She might as well mistake black for white as to believe that Lienhard cared for her. To no one save his fair young wife would he grant even the smallest ray of the love of which he was doubtless capable, and in which she beheld the sun that dispensed life and light. She had learned this, for he had often met her in Frau Sophia's house since his father's funeral. The child of the highway had never been taught to conceal her feelings and maintain timid reserve. Her eyes had told him eloquently enough, first her deep sympathy, and afterward the emotions which so passionately stirred her heart. Had the feelings which her glances were intended to reveal passed merely for the ardent gratitude of an impassioned soul?

Gratitude! For what?

His lukewarm interest had tempted her from a free, gay life, full of constant excitement, into the oppressive, wearisome monotony of this quiet house, where she was dying of ennui. How narrow, how petty, how tiresome everything seemed, and what she had bartered for it was the world, the whole wide, wide world. As the chicken lured the fox, the hope of satisfying the fervent longing of her heart, though even once and for a few brief moments, had brought her into the snare. But the fire which burned within had not been extinguished. An icy wind had fanned the flames till they blazed higher and higher, threatening her destruction.

Frau Schurstab had made her attend church and go to the confessional. But the mass, whose meaning she did not understand, offered no solace to the soul which yearned for love alone. Besides, it wearied her to remain so long in the same place, and the confession forced the girl, who had never shrunk from honestly expressing what she felt, into deception. The priest to whom she was taken was a frequent visitor at the Schurstab house, and she would have died ere she would have confided to him the secret of her heart. Besides, to her the feeling which animated her was no sin. She had not summoned it. It had taken possession of her against her will and harmed no one except herself, not even the wife who was so sure of her husband. How could she have presumed to dispute with her the possession of Herr Lienhard's love? Yet it seemed an insult that Frau Katharina had no fear that she could menace her happiness. Could the former know that Kuni would have been content with so little—a tender impulse of his heart, a kiss, a hasty embrace? That would do the other no injury. In the circles whence she had been brought no one grudged another such things. How little, she thought, would have been taken from the wealthy Katharina by the trifling gift which would have restored to her happiness and peace. The fact that Lienhard, though he never failed to notice her, would not understand, and always maintained the same pleasant, aristocratic reserve of manner, she sometimes attributed to fear, sometimes to cruelty, sometimes to arrogance; she would not believe that he saw in her only a person otherwise indifferent to him, whom he wished to accustom to the mode of life which he and his friends believed to be the right path, pleasing in the sight of God. Love, feminine vanity, the need of approval, her own pride—all opposed this view.

When the last snow of winter had melted, and the spring sunshine of April was unfolding the green leafage and opening bright flowers in the meadows, the hedges, the woods, and the gardens, she found the new home which she had entered during the frosts of February, and whose solid walls excluded every breath of air, more and more unendurable. A gnawing feeling of homesickness for the free out-of-door life, the wandering from place to place, the careless, untrammelled people to whom she belonged, took possession of her. She felt as though everything which surrounded her was too small, the house, the apartments, her own chamber, nay, her very clothing. Only the hope of the first token that Lienhard was not so cold and unconquerable as he seemed, that she would at last constrain him to pass the barrier which separated them, still detained her.

Then came the day when, to avoid answering his question whether she needed anything, she had gone into the garden. Before reaching the children, who were playing among the crocuses and tulips, she had said to herself that she must leave this house—it was foolish, nay mad, to continue to cherish the hope which had brought her hither. She would suffer keenly in tearing it from her heart, but a wild delight seized her at the thought that this imprisonment would soon be over, that she would be free once more, entirely her own mistress, released from every restraint and consideration. How rapturous was the idea that she would soon be roving through the fields and woods again with gay, reckless companions! Was there anything more pleasurable than to forget herself, and devote her whole soul to the execution of some difficult and dangerous feat, to attract a thousand eyes by her bewitching grace, and, sustained by her enthusiasm, force a thousand hearts to throb anxiously and give loud applause as she flew over the rope?

Never had the children seen her more extravagantly gay than after her resolve to leave them. Yet when, at a late hour, Kuni went to bed, the old housekeeper heard her weeping so piteously in her chamber that she rose to ask what had happened. But the girl did not even open her door, and declared that she had probably had the nightmare.

During the next few days she sometimes appeared more cheerful and docile, sometimes more dull and troubled than her household companions had ever seen her. Frau Schurstab shook her head over her protegee's varying moods. But when the month of May began, and Lienhard told his aunt that Loni, who had only remained in Nuremberg during Lent to spend the time when all public performances were prohibited, had applied to the Council for permission to give exhibitions with his company Easter week in the Haller Meadows, the matron was troubled about her protegee's peace of mind. Her nephew had had the same thought, and advised her to move to her country estate, that Kuni might see and hear nothing of the jugglers; but she had noticed the clown with other members of the company, as they passed through the streets on foot and mounted on horses and donkeys, inviting the people, with blare of trumpets and beating of drums, to witness the wonderful feats which Loni's famous band of artists would perform.

Then Kuni packed her bundle. But when she heard the next morning that, before going to the country, Frau Schurstab would attend the christening of her youngest grandson, and spend the whole day with the daughter who was the little boy's mother, she untied it.

One sunny May morning she was left alone, as she had expected. She could not be invited to the ceremony with the other guests, and she would not join the servants. The housekeeper and most of the men and maids had accompanied their mistress to help in the kitchen and to wait upon the visitors. Deep silence reigned throughout the great empty house, but Kuni's heart had never throbbed so loudly. If Lienhard came now, her fate would be decided, and she knew that he must come. Just before noon, he really did rap with the knocker on the outer door. He wanted the christening gift, which Frau Schurstab had forgotten to take for the infant. The money was in the chest in the matron's room. Kuni led the way. The house seemed to reel around her as she went up the stairs behind him. The next moment, she felt, must decide her destiny.

Now he laid his hand upon the doorknob, now he opened the door. The widow's chamber was before her. Thick silk curtains shut out the bright May sunshine from the quiet room. How warm and pleasant it was!

She already saw herself in imagination kneeling by his side before the chest to help him search. While doing so, his fingers might touch hers, perhaps her hair might brush against his. But, instead of entering, he turned to her with careless unconcern, saying:

"It is fortunate that I have found you alone. Will you do me a favour, girl?"

He had intended to ask her to help him prepare a surprise for his aunt. The day after to-morrow was Frau Sophia Schurstab's birthday. Early in the morning she must find among her feathered favourites a pair of rare India fowls, which he had received from Venice.

As Kuni did not instantly assent, because the wild tumult of her blood paralyzed her tongue, he noticed her confusion, and in an encouraging tone, gaily continued:

"What I have to ask is not too difficult." As he spoke he passed his hand kindly over her dark hair, just as he had done a few months before in the Town Hall.

Then the blood mounted to her brain. Clasping his right hand, beneath whose touch she had just trembled, in both her own, she passionately exclaimed:

"Ask whatever you desire. If you wanted to trample my heart under your feet, I would not stir."

A look of ardent love from her sparkling blue eyes accompanied the words; but he had withdrawn his hand in astonishment, and raised a lofty barrier between them by answering coldly and sternly, "Keep the heart and your dainty self for the equerry Seifried who is an honest man."

The advice, and the lofty austerity with which it was given, pierced Kuni like the thrust of a dagger. Yet she succeeded controlling herself, and, without a word reply, preceded the harsh man into the sleeping room and silently, tearlessly, pointed the chest. When he had taken out the money, she bowed hastily and ran down the stairs.

Probably she heard him call her name more than three times; doubtless, afterward she fancied that she remembered how his voice had sounded in beseeching, tender, at last even imperious tones through the empty corridors; but she did not turn, and hurried into her room.

CHAPTER V

When, on the evening of the christening day, Lienhard accompanied his aunt home, Kuni was nowhere to be found. Frau Sophia discovered in her chamber every article of clothing which she had obtained for her, even the beaver cap, the prayer-book, and the rosary which she had given. The young burgomaster, at her request, went to the manager of the rope-dancers, Loni, the next morning, but the latter asserted that he knew nothing about the girl. The truth was that he had sent her to Wurzburg with part of his company.

From that time she had remained with the ropedancers. At first the master had watched her carefully, that she might not run away again. But he soon perceived this to be unnecessary; for he had never found any member of the company more zealous, or seen one make more progress in the art. Now the only point was to keep her out of the way of other rope-dancers, English proprietors of circus companies, as well as the numerous knights and gentlemen who tried to take her from him. Her name had become famous. When the crier proclaimed that the "flying maiden" would ascend the rope to the steeple, Loni was sure of a great crowd of spectators. Among her own profession she had obtained the nickname of crazy Kuni.

Yet even at that time, and in the midst of the freest intercourse with German, Spanish, and other officers in Flanders and Brabant, young knights and light-hearted priests on the Rhine, the Main, the Danube, the Weser, and the Elbe, whose purses the pretty, vivacious girl, with the shining raven hair and bright blue eyes, the mistress of her art, seemed to their owners worthy to empty, she had by no means forgotten Lienhard. This wrought mischief to many a gay gentleman of aristocratic lineage in the great imperial and commercial cities; for it afforded Kuni special pleasure to try her power upon Lienhard's equals in rank. When she went on with the company, more than one patrician had good reason to remember her with regret; for she, who shared the lion's portion of her earnings with her companions or flung it to the poor, was insatiably avaricious toward these admirers.

The weaker she found many of them, the higher, in her opinion, rose the image of him who had made her feel his manly strength of resistance so cruelly. His stern, inexorable nature seemed to her worthy of hate, yet for three whole years the longing for him scarcely left her heart at peace an hour.

During this whole period she had not met him. Not until after she had come to Augsburg, where Loni's company was to give several performances before the assembled Reichstag, did she see him again. Once she even succeeded in attracting his gaze, and this was done in a way which afforded her great satisfaction. His beautiful wife, clad in costly velvet robes, was walking by his side with eyes decorously downcast; but he had surely recognised her—there was no doubt of that. Yet he omitted to inform his wife, even by a look, whom he had met here. Kuni watched the proud couple a long time, and, with the keen insight of a loving heart, told herself that he would have pointed her out to Frau Katharina, if he did not remember her in some way—either in kindness or in anger.

This little discovery had sufficed to transfigure, as it were, the rest of the day, and awaken a throng of new hopes and questions.

Even now she did not desire to win Frau Katharina's husband from her. She freely acknowledged that the other's beauty was tenfold greater than her own; but whether the gifts of love which the woman with the cloudless, aristocratic composure could offer to her husband were not like the beggar's pence, compared with the overflowing treasure of ardent passion which she cherished for Lienhard, was a question to which she believed there could be but a single answer. Was this lady, restricted by a thousand petty scruples, as well as by her stiff, heavy gala robes, a genuine woman at all? Ah! if he would only for once cast aside the foolish considerations which prevented him also from being a genuine man, clasp her, whom he knew was his own, in his arms, and hold her as long as he desired, he should learn what a strong, free, fearless woman, whose pliant limbs were as unfettered as her heart, could bestow upon him to whom she gave all the love that she possessed! And he must want something of her which was to be concealed from the wife. She could not be mistaken. She had never been deceived in a presentiment that was so positive. Ever since she reached Augsburg, an inner voice had told her— and old Brigitta's cards confirmed it—that the destiny of her life would be decided here, and he alone held her weal and woe in his hand.

Yet she had misinterpreted his conduct to his wife. In spite of the finery which Kuni owed to the generosity of the Knight of Neckerfels, who was then a suitor for her favour, Lienhard had recognised her. The sight recalled their last meeting and its painful termination, and therefore he had omitted to attract Frau Katharina's attention to her immediately. But, ere Kuni disappeared, he had repaired the oversight, and both desired to ascertain the fate of their former charge. True, the wish could not be instantly fulfilled, for Lienhard's time and strength were wholly claimed by the mission intrusted to him by the Emperor and the Council.

The next afternoon Kuni ascended the rope to the steeple in the presence of many princes and dignitaries. Firmly as ever she moved along the rope stretched through the wooden stay behind her, holding the balancing pole as she went. The clapping of hands and shouts of applause with which the crowd greeted "the flying maiden" led her to kiss her hand to the right and the left, and bow to the stand which had been erected for the crowned heads, counts, nobles, and their wives. In doing so, she looked down at the aristocratic spectators to ascertain whether the Emperor and one other were among them. In spite of the height of the topmost window of the steeple where she stood, her keen eyes showed her that Maximilian's seat was still vacant. As it was hung with purple draperies and richly garlanded, the monarch was evidently expected. This pleased her, and her heart throbbed faster as she saw on the stand all the nobles who were entitled to admittance to the lists of a tournament, and, in the front row, the man whose presence she most desired. At Lienhard's right sat his dazzlingly beautiful wife, adorned with plumes and the most superb gold ornaments; at his left was a maiden of extremely peculiar charm. According to years she was still a child, but her delicate, mobile features had a mature expression, which sometimes gave her a precocious air of superiority. The cut of her white robe and the little laurel wreath on her brown curls reminded Kuni of the pagan Genius on an ancient work of marble which she had seen in Verona. Neither the girl's age nor her light, airy costume harmonized with her surroundings; for the maids and matrons near her were all far beyond childhood, and wore the richest holiday costumes of heavy brocades and velvets. The huge puffs on the upper part of the sleeves touched the cheeks of many of the wearers, and the lace ruffs on the stiff collars rendered it easy, it is true, to maintain their aristocratic, haughty dignity, but prevented any free, swift movement.

The young girl who, as Kuni afterward learned, was the daughter of Conrad Peutinger, of Augsburg, whom she had again seen that day in The Blue Pike, was then eleven years old. She was sometimes thought to be fifteen or even sixteen; her mobile face did not retain the same expression a single instant. When the smile which gave her a childlike appearance vanished, and any earnest feeling stirred her soul, she really resembled a mature maiden. What a brilliant, versatile intellect must animate this remarkable creature! Lienhard, shrewd and highly educated as he was, seemed to be completely absorbed in his neighbour; nay, in his animated conversation with her he entirely forgot the beautiful wife at his side; at least, while Kuni looked down at him, he did not bestow a single glance upon her. Now he shook his finger mischievously at the child, but he seemed to be seeking, in mingled amusement and perplexity, to find a fitting answer. And how brightly Lienhard's eyes sparkled as he fairly hung upon the sweet red lips of the little marvel at his left—the heart side! A few minutes had sufficed to show the ropedancer all this, and suggest the question whether it was possible that the most faithful of husbands would thus basely neglect, for the sake of a child, the young wife whom he had won in spite of the hardest obstacles, on whose account he had so coldly and cruelly rejected her, the object of so much wooing, and who, this very day, was the fairest of all the beautiful ladies who surrounded her.

In an instant her active mind transported her to the soul of the hitherto favoured wife of the man whom she loved, and her strangely constituted woman's heart filled with resentment against the young creature below, who had not even attained womanhood, and yet seemed to gain, without effort, the prize for which she had vainly striven with painful longing.

She, whose heart had remained free from jealousy of the woman who stood between her and the man she loved, like a solid bulwark erected by Fate itself, was now suddenly overmastered by this passion.

Yet she did not turn against the person to whom Lienhard belonged, as he did to the city, or to his own family, and who was united to him by the will of Heaven, but against the mysterious young creature at his side, who changed with every passing moment.

This child—no, this maiden—must be a being of some special nature. Like the sirens of whom she had heard, she possessed the mysterious, enviable power of conquering the iron resistance of even the strongest man.

Like a flash of lightning, Kuni, whose kind heart cherished resentment against few and wished no one any evil, suddenly felt an ardent desire to drive the little witch from Lienhard's side, even by force, if necessary. Had she held a thunderbolt instead of a balance pole, she would gladly have struck down the treacherous child from her height—not only because this enchantress had so quickly won that for which she had vainly yearned, alas! how long, but because it pierced her very heart to see Frau Katharina's happiness clouded, nay, perhaps destroyed. A bitterness usually alien to her light, gay nature had taken possession of her, as, with the last glance she cast at Lienhard, she saw him bend low over the child and, with fiery ardour, whisper something which transformed the delicate pink flush in her cheeks to the hue of the poppy.

Yes, the ropedancer was jealous of the laurel-crowned child. She, who cared so little for law and duty, virtue and morality, now felt offended, wounded, tortured by Lienhard's conduct. But there was no time to ponder over the reason now. She had already delayed too long ere moving forward.

Yet even calm reflection would not have revealed the right answer to the problem. How could she have suspected that what stirred her passionate soul so fiercely was grief at the sight of the man whom she had regarded as the stronghold of integrity, the possessor of the firmest will, the soul of inviolable fidelity, succumbing here, before the eyes of all, like a dissolute weakling, to the seductive arts of an immature kobold? These two, who gave to her, the orphaned vagrant, surrounded by unbridled recklessness, physical and mental misery, a proof that there was still in marriage real love and a happiness secure from every assault, were now, before her eyes, placing themselves on the same plane with the miserable couples whom she met everywhere. She could not have expressed her emotions in words, but she vaguely felt that the world had become poorer, and that henceforth she must think of something more trivial when she tried to imagine the pure happiness which mortals are permitted to enjoy. She had seen the blossoms stripped from the scanty remnant of her faith in truth and goodness, which had begun to bloom afresh in her heart through the characters of this pair whose marriage procession she had watched.

Loni had been beckoning a long time; now he waved his gay handkerchief still more impatiently, and she moved on.

Her lips forced themselves into the customary smile with difficulty. Tripping forward was an easy matter for one so free from dizziness. She only carried the pole because it was customary to begin with the least difficult feats. Yet, while gracefully placing one foot before the other, she said to herself—safe as she felt—that, while so much agitated, she would be wiser not to look down again into the depths below. She did avoid it, and with a swift run gained the end of the rope without effort, and went up and down it a second time.

While, on reaching the end of her walk, she was chalking her soles again, the applause which had accompanied her during her dangerous pilgrimage still rose to her ears, and came-most loudly of all from the stand where Lienhard sat among the distinguished spectators. He, too, had clapped his hands lustily, and shouted, "Bravo!" Never had he beheld any ropedancer display so much grace, strength, and daring. His modest protegee had become a magnificently developed woman. How could he have imagined that the unfortunate young creature whom he had saved from disgrace would show such courage, such rare skill?

He confided his feelings, and the fact that he knew the artist, to his young neighbour, but she had turned deadly pale and lowered her eyes. While looking on she had felt as though she herself was in danger of falling into the depths. Giddiness had seized her, and her heart, whose tendency to disease had long awakened the apprehension of the physicians, contracted convulsively. The sight of a fellow-being hovering in mortal peril above her head seemed unendurable. Not until she followed Lienhard's advice and avoided looking up, did she regain her calmness. Her changeful temperament soon recovered its former cheerfulness, and the friend at her side to whom the lovely child, with her precocious mental development, appeared like the fairest marvel, took care, often as he himself looked upward, that she should be guarded from a second attack of weakness.

The storm of applause from below, in which Lienhard also joined, fanned the flames of desire for admiration in Kuni's breast to a fiery glow. She would show him, too, what she could do—compel him to applaud her. She would force him away from the little temptress, and oblige him to gaze up at her whose art—she learned this daily—possessed the power to fix the attention of spectators like the thrall of the basilisk's eye. When on the rope she was no insignificant personage. He should tremble for her as did the gray-haired, scarred captain of the foot soldiers, Mannsbach, the day before yesterday. He had told her that his heart had throbbed more anxiously during her daring feats than on the bloodiest field of battle.

She moved forward more swiftly to the time of the lively dancing tune which the city pipers were playing. Midway along the rope she turned, ran back to the cross-shaped trestle at the steeple window, handed the balancing pole to Loni, and received a cage filled with doves. Each one bore around its neck a note containing an expression of homage to the Emperor Maximilian, and they were all trained to alight near the richly decorated throne which was now occupied by the chivalrous monarch. The clown who, with a comical show of respect, offered her what she needed for her next feat, told her this.

Loni, sure of being heard by no unbidden ear, called to her from the window:

"Art is honoured to-day, my girl."

The clown added jocosely:

"Who else was ever permitted to walk over the anointed head of our lord the Emperor?"

But Kuni would not have needed such encouragement. Doubtless she felt flattered by the consciousness of attracting even the sovereign's glance, but what she intended to do immediately was for the purpose of compelling another person to watch her steps with fear and admiration. Crossing her feet, she threw back her garlanded head and drew a long breath. Then she hastily straightened herself, and with the bird cage in one hand and the winged staff of Mercury, which the clown had handed to her, in the other, she advanced to the centre of the rope. There she opened the cage as steadily as if she had been standing on the floor of her own room. The birds fluttered through the little door and went, with a swift flight, directly to their goal. Then, below and beside her, from every place occupied by spectators, and from hundreds of windows, rose thunders of applause; but it seemed to her as if the roaring of the surging sea was in her ears. Her heart throbbed under her pink silk bodice like an iron hammer, and in the proud consciousness of having probably attained already what she desired, and, besides thousands of other eyes, fixed Lienhard's upon her as if with chains and bonds, she was seized with the ambitious desire to accomplish something still more amazing. The man to whom her heart clung, the Emperor, the countless multitude below, were all at this time subject to her in heart and mind. They could think and feel nothing except what concerned her, her art, and her fate. She could and would show to Lienhard, to the Emperor, to all, what they had never witnessed. They should turn faint with sympathizing anxiety. She would make then realize what genuine art, skill, and daring could accomplish. Everything else, even the desire for applause, was forgotten. Though her performance might be called only a perilous feat, she felt it to be true, genuine art. Her whole soul was merged in the desire to execute, boldly and yet gracefully, the greatest and most perfect performance attainable by a ropedancer. With beads of perspiration on her brow, and eyes uplifted, she threw the cage aside, swung her Mercury staff aloft, and danced along the rope in waltz time, as though borne by the gods of the wind. Whirling swiftly around, her slender figure darted in graceful curves from one end of the narrow path to the other. Then the applause reached the degree of enthusiastic madness which she desired; even Loni clapped his hands from the steeple window. She had never seen him do this to any of the company. Yes, she must have accomplished her purpose well; but she would show him and the others something still more wonderful. What she had just done was capable of many additional feats; she had tried it.

With fluttering hands and pulses she instantly loosed from her panting bosom and her hips the garland of roses and leaves twined about the upper portion of her body, and swung it around her in graceful curves as she knelt and rose on the rope.

She had often jumped rope on the low rope, turning completely around so that she faced the other way. To repeat this performance on the one stretched to the steeple would certainly not be expected from her or from any other. Suppose she should use the garland as a rope and venture to leap over it on this giddy height? Suppose she should even succeed in turning around? The rope was firm. If her plan was successful, she would have accomplished something unprecedented; if she failed—if, while turning, she lost her balance—her scanty stock of pleasure here below would be over, and also her great grief and insatiable yearning. One thing was certain: Lienhard would watch her breathlessly, nay, tremble for her. Perhaps it was too much to hope that he would mourn her sincerely, should the leap cost her life; but he would surely pity her, and he could never forget the moment of the fall, and therefore herself. Loni would tear the gold circlet from his dyed black locks and, in his exaggerated manner, call himself a son of misfortune, and her the greatest artist who had ever trodden the rope. All Augsburg, all the dignitaries of the realm, even the Emperor, would pity her, and the end of her life would be as proud and as renowned as that of the chivalrous hero who dies victor on the stricken field. If the early part of her life had been insignificant and wretched, its close should be grand and beautiful.

Long consideration was foreign to Kuni's nature. While these thoughts were darting with the speed of lightning through her excited brain, she stripped from the garland, with the presence of mind which her calling teaches even in serious peril, the roses which might have caught her feet, and swung it in a wide circle above her. Then nimbly, yet careful to maintain in every movement the grace without which the most difficult feat would have seemed to her valueless, she summoned all the strength and caution she possessed, went forward at a run, and—she did not know herself just how it was done—dared the leap over the rope once, twice, and the third and fourth time even accomplished the turn successfully. It had not once cost her an effort to maintain her balance.

Again she saw Loni clapping his hands at the window, and the acclamations of the crowd, which echoed like peals of thunder from the lofty, gable- roofed houses, informed her that the boldness of the venture and the skill with which she had performed it were appreciated by these spectators. True, she could not distinguish the voice of any individual, but she thought she knew that Lienhard was one of those who shouted "Bravo!" and clapped most loudly. He must have perceived now that she was something more than a poor thief of a rosary, a useless bread-eater in the Schurstab household.

She straightened the garland again and, while preparing to take another run, repeat the feat, and, if her buoyancy held out, try to whirl around twice, which she had never failed to accomplish on the low rope, she could not resist the temptation of casting a hasty glance at Lienhard; she had never ascended to the steeple without looking at him.

Secure of herself, in the glad conciousness of success, she gazed down.

There sat the illustrious Maximilian, still clapping his hands. Gratefully, yet with a passionate desire for fresh applause, the resolve to show him the very best which she could accomplish was strengthened. But the next moment the blood faded from her slightly rouged cheeks, for Lienhard—was it possible, was it imaginable?—Lienhard Groland was not looking up at her! Without moving his hands or vouchsafing her a single glance, he was gazing into the face of the little wearer of the laurel wreath, with whom he was eagerly talking. He was under her thrall, body and soul. Yet it could not be, she could not have seen distinctly. She must look down once more, to correct the error. She did so, and a torturing anguish seized her heart. He was chatting with the child as before; nay, with still more warmth. As he now saw nothing which was happening upon the rope, he had probably also failed to heed what she had performed, dared, accomplished, mainly for his sake, at the peril of her life, on the dizzy height. His wife was still clapping her hands at his side, but Lienhard, as though deaf and blind to everything else, was gazing at the page which the miserable little elf was just giving him. There was certainly writing on it—perhaps a charm which rendered him subject to her. How else could he have brought himself to overlook so unkindly herself and her art—the best she had to bestow—for the sake of this child?

Then, besides the keenest sorrow, a fierce, burning hate took possession of her soul.

She had not appealed to her saint for years; but now, in a brief, ejaculatory prayer, she besought her to drive this child from Lienhard, punish her with misery, suffering, and destruction. A sharp pang which she had never before experienced pierced her to the heart. The pure, sunny air which she inhaled on her lofty height seemed like acrid smoke, and forced tears into the eyes which had not wept for many a long day.

As, not knowing exactly what she was doing, with her ears deafened by the shouts of the crowd, among whom Lienhard now, with anxious suspense, watched her every movement, she again raised the rope and prepared to spring, she fancied that her narrow path rose higher and higher. One more step, and suddenly, with Loui's shriek of horror and the clown's terrified "Jesus and Mary, she is falling!" ringing on the air, she felt as if the rope had parted directly in front of her. Then a hurricane appeared to howl around her, bearing her away she knew not whither. It seemed as though the tempest had seized the ends of the rope, and was dealing terrible blows with them upon her shoulders, her back, and her feet. Meanwhile the little wearer of the wreath was lying on a black cloud opposite to her at Lienhard's feet.

She still held the sheet in her hand, and was shouting to the angry elements the magic formulas which it contained. Their power Kuni knew it—had unchained them. Lienhard's deep voice mingled with her furious cries until the roar of the sea, on whose rocky shore the hurricane must have dashed her, drowned every other sound, and rolled over her, sometimes in scorching crimson, sometimes in icy crystal waves. Then, for a long time, she saw and heard nothing more.

When her deadened imagination again began to stir, she fancied that she was struggling with a huge crab, which was cutting her foot with shears. The little elf was urging it on, as the huntsmen cheer the hounds. The pain and hate she felt would have been intolerable if Lienhard had made common cause with the terrible child. But he reproved her conduct, and even struggled with the kobold who tried to prevent his releasing her from the crab. The elf proved stronger than he. The terrible shears continued to torture her. The more she suffered, the more eagerly Lienhard seemed trying to help her, and this soothed her and blended a sweet sense of comfort with the burning pain.

CHAPTER VI

Kuni remained under the spell of these delusions for many days and nights. When she at last regained her senses, she was lying on a plain couch in a long, whitewashed hall. The well-scoured floor was strewn with sand and pine needles. Other beds stood beside hers. On one wall hung a large wooden crucifix, painted with glaring colours; on the other a touching picture of the Mater Dolorosa, with the swords in her heart, looked down upon her.

Beside Kuni's pallet stood a Gray Sister and an elderly man, evidently a physician. His long black robe, tall dark cap, and gold headed cane bore witness to it. Bending forward, with eyeglasses on his prominent nose, he gazed intently into her face.

Her return to consciousness seemed to please him, and he showed himself to be a kind, experienced leech. With tireless solicitude he strove to cure the numerous injuries which she had received, and she soon learned through him and the nun, that she had fallen from the rope and escaped death as if by a miracle. The triumphal arch under her, and the garlands which decorated the wooden structure, had caught her before she touched the pavement. True, her right leg was broken, and it had been necessary to amputate her left foot in order to save her life. Many a wound and slash on her breast and head also needed healing, and her greatest ornament, her long, thick, dark hair, had been cut off.

Why had they called her, the ropedancer, back to a life which henceforward could offer her nothing save want and cruel suffering? She uttered this reproach to her preservers very indignantly; but as the physician saw her eating a bunch of grapes with much enjoyment, he asked if this pleasure did not suffice to make her rejoice over the preservation of her existence. There were a thousand similar gifts of God, which scarcely seemed worthy of notice, yet in the aggregate outweighed a great sorrow which, moreover, habit daily diminished.

The Sister tried, by other arguments, to reconcile her to the life which had been preserved, but the words her devout heart inspired and which were intended for a pious soul, produced little influence upon the neglected child of the highroad. Kuni felt most deeply the reference to the sorely afflicted Mother of God. If such sorrow had been sent to the noblest and purest of mortals, through whom God had deigned to give his divine Son to the world, what grief could be too great for her, the wandering vagabond? She often silently repeated this to herself; yet only too frequently her impetuous heart rebelled against the misery which she felt that she would encounter. But many weeks were to pass before she recovered; a severe relapse again endangered her life.

During the first days of illness she had talked to Lienhard in her fevered visions, called him by name, and warned him against the spiteful elf who would ruin him. Frequently, too, oaths and horrible, coarse imprecations, such as are heard only from the mouths of the vagrants among whom she had grown to womanhood, fell from her burning lips. When she improved, the leech asked in the jesting tone which elderly men are fond of using to young women whose heart secrets they think they have detected, what wrong her lover had done her. The Sister, nay, even the abbess, wished to learn what she meant by the wicked witch whom she had mentioned with such terrible curses during the ravings of the fever, but she made no reply. In fact, she said very little, and her nurses thought her a reserved creature with an obdurate nature; for she obstinately rejected the consolations of religion.

Only to her confessor, a kind old priest, who knew how to discover the best qualities in every one, did she open her heart so far as to reveal that she loved the husband of another and had once wished evil, ay, the very worst evil, to a neighbour. But since the sin had been committed only in thought, the kindly guardian of her conscience was quickly disposed to grant her absolution if, as a penance, she would repeat a goodly number of paternosters and undertake a pilgrimage. If she had had sound feet, she ought to have journeyed to Santiago di Compostella; but, since her condition precluded this, a visit to Altotting in Bavaria would suffice. But Kuni by no means desired any mitigation of the penance. She silently resolved to undertake the pilgrimage to Compostella, at the World's End,—[Cape Finisterre]—in distant Spain, though she did not know how it would be possible to accomplish this with her mutilated foot. Not even to her kind confessor did she reveal this design. The girl who had relied upon herself from childhood, needed no explanation, no confidante.

Therefore, during the long days and nights which she was obliged to spend in bed, she pondered still more constantly upon her own past. That she had been drawn and was still attracted to Lienhard with resistless power, was true; yet whom, save herself, had this wounded or injured? On the other hand, it had assuredly been a heavy sin that she had called down such terrible curses upon the child. Still, even now she might have had good reason to execrate the wearer of the wreath; for she alone, not Lienhard, was the sole cause of her misfortune. Her prayer on the rope that the saints would destroy the hated child, and the idea which then occupied her mind, that she was really a grown maiden, whose elfin delicacy of figure was due to her being one of the fays or elves mentioned in the fairy tales, had made a deep impression upon her memory.

Whenever she thought of that supplication she again felt the bitterness she had tasted on the rope. Though she believed herself justified in hating the little mischief-maker, the prayer uttered before her fall did not burden her soul much less heavily than a crime. Suppose the Sister was right, and that the saints heard every earnest petition?

She shuddered at the thought. The child was so young, so delicate. Though she had caused her misfortune, the evil was not done intentionally. Such thoughts often induced Kuni to clasp her hands and pray to the saint not to fulfil the prayer she uttered at that time; but she did not continue the petition long, a secret voice whispered that every living creature—man and beast—felt the impulse to inflict a similar pang on those who caused suffering, and that she, who believed the whole world wicked, need not be better than the rest.

Meanwhile she longed more and more eagerly to know the name of the little creature that had brought so much trouble upon her, and whether she was still forcing herself between Lienhard and his beautiful wife.

As soon as she was able to talk again, she began her inquiries. The Sister, who was entirely absorbed in her calling and never left the scene of her wearisome toil, had little to tell; but the leech and the priest, in reply to her questions concerning what had happened during the period of her unconsciousness, informed her that the Emperor had ordered that she should receive the most careful nursing, and had bestowed a donation upon the convent for the purpose. He had thought of her future, too. When she recovered, she would have the five heller pounds which the generous sovereign had left for her as a partial compensation for the injuries sustained while employing her rare skill for the delight of the multitude and, above all, himself. A wealthy Nuremberg Honourable, Lienhard Groland, a member of the Council, had also interested himself in her and deposited the same amount with the abbess, in case she should recover the use of her limbs and did not prefer to spend the remainder of her life here, though only as a lay sister. In that case he would be ready to defray the cost of admission.

"That the lofty convent walls might rise between him and the sight of me!" Kuni said to herself at this information, with a bitter smile. On the—other hand, her eyes filled with tears of genuine emotion and sincere shame, when she learned from the leech that Herr Lienhard Groland's lovely wife had come daily to the convent to inquire about her, and had even honoured her couch with a visit several times. She did not remain absent until one day, in the noble lady's presence, Kuni, when her fever was fiercest, loaded the wearer of the wreath, whom her delirium often brought before her as a nightmare, with the most savage and blasphemous curses. The gracious young wife was overwhelmed with horror, which had doubtless prevented her return, unless her absence was due to departure from the city. Besides, she had committed the care of inquiring about her convalescence to an aristocratic friend in Augsburg, the wife of the learned city clerk, Doctor Peutinger, a member of the famous Welser family of Augsburg. The latter had often inquired for her in person, until the illness of her own dear child had kept her at home. Yet, in spite of this, her housekeeper had appeared the day before to inform the abbess that, if the injured girl should recover and wished to lead a respectable life in future, she might be sure of a welcome and easy duties in her own household. This surely ought to be a great comfort to Kuni, the physician added; for she could no longer pursue rope-dancing, and the Peutingers were lavishly endowed with worldly goods and intellectual gifts, and, besides, were people of genuine Christian spirit. The convent, too, would be ready to receive her—the abbess had told him so—if Herr Groland, of Nuremberg, kept his promise of paying her admission dues.

All these things awakened a new world of thoughts and feelings in the convalescent. That they ought, above all, to have aroused sincere gratitude, she felt keenly, yet she could not succeed in being especially thankful. It would be doing Lienhard a favour, she repeated to herself, if she should enter a convent, and she would rather have sought shelter in a lion's den than under the Peutinger roof. She had been informed the day before that the city clerk's wife was the mother of the child upon whom she had called down misfortune and death.

The keeper of an Augsburg bath-house, who had burned herself with boiling water, occupied the next bed. She was recovering, and was a talkative woman, whose intrusive loquacity at first annoyed Kuni, nay, when she could not silence it, caused her pain. But her conversation soon revealed that she knew every stick and stone in her native city. Kuni availed herself of this, and did not need to ask many questions to learn everything that she desired to know about the little begarlanded elf.

She was Juliane, the young daughter of Herr Conrad Peutinger, the city clerk—a girl of unusual cleverness, and a degree of learning never before found in a child eleven years old. The bath-house keeper had many wonderful stories to relate of her remarkable wisdom, with which even highly educated men could not vie. In doing so, she blamed the father and mother, who had been unnatural parents to the charming child; for to make the marvel complete, and to gratify their own vanity, they had taxed the little girl's mind with such foolish strenuousness that the frail body suffered. She had heard this in her own bath-house from the lips of the child's aunt and from other distinguished friends of the Welsers and Peutingers. Unfortunately, these sensible women proved to have been right; for soon after the close of the Reichstag, Juliane was attacked by a lingering illness, from which rumour now asserted that she would never recover. Some people even regarded the little girl's sickness as a just punishment of God, to whom the constant devotion of the father and his young daughter to the old pagans and their ungodly writings must have given grave offence.

This news increased to the utmost the anxiety from which Kuni had long suffered. Often as she thought of Lienhard, she remembered still more frequently that it was she, who had prayed for sickness to visit the child of a mother, who had so kindly offered her, the strolling player, whom good women usually shunned, the shelter of her distinguished house.

The consciousness of owing a debt of gratitude to those, against whom she had sinned so heavily, oppressed her. The kind proposal of the sick child's mother seemed like a mockery. It was painful even to hear the name of Peutinger.

Besides, the further she advanced toward recovery, the more unendurable appeared the absence of liberty. The kind efforts of the abbess to keep her in the cloister, and teach her to make herself useful there by sewing, were unsuccessful; for she could not turn the spinning wheel on account of her amputated foot, and she had neither inclination nor patience for the finer branches of needlework.

Those who charged her with a lamentable lack of perseverance were right; the linen which she began to hem fell into her lap only too soon. When her eyes—which could see nothing here except a small walled yard—closed while she was working, the others thought that she was asleep; but her mind remained awake, though she had lowered her lids, and it wandered restlessly over valleys rivers, and mountains through the wide, wide world. She saw herself in imagination travelling along the highway with nimble jugglers merry musicians, and other care-free vagrant folk, instead of plying the needle. Even the whirling dust, the rushing wind, and the refreshing rain outside seemed desirable compared with the heavy convent air impregnated by a perpetual odour of lavender.

When at last, in the month of March, little Afra, the fair-haired niece of the portress, brought her the first snowdrop, and Kuni saw a pair of starlings enter the box on the budding linden before her window, she could no longer bear her imprisonment in the convent.

Within these walls she must fade, perhaps die and return to dust. In spite of all the warnings, representations, entreaties, and promises of those who—she gratefully perceived it—meant well toward her, she persisted in her desire to be dismissed, to live out of doors as she had always done. At last they paid her what was due, but she accepted only the Emperor's bounty, proudly refusing Lienhard Groland's money, earnestly as she was urged to add it to the other and to the viaticum bestowed by the nuns.

CHAPTER VII

The April sun was shining brightly when the convent gates closed behind Kuni. The lindens in the square were already putting forth young leaves, the birds were singing, and her heart swelled more joyously than it had done for many years.

True, the cough which had tormented her all winter attacked her in the shady cloister, but she had learned to use her wooden foot, and with a cane in one hand and her little bundle in the other she moved sturdily on. After making her pilgrimage to Compostella, she intended to seek her old employer, Loni. Perhaps he could give her a place as crier, or if the cough prevented that, in collecting the money or training the children. He was a kind-hearted man. If he were even tolerably prosperous he would certainly let her travel with the band, and give the girl who was injured in his service the bit of food she required. Besides, in former days, when she scattered gold with lavish hands, he had predicted what had now befallen her, and when he left Augsburg he had asked the nuns to tell her that if she should ever be in want she must remember Loni.

With the Emperor's five heller pounds, and the two florins which she had received as a viaticum from the convent, she could journey a long distance through the world; for there were plenty of carriers and travellers with carts and wagons who would take her for a trifle, and the vagabonds on the highway rarely left people like her in the lurch.

Probably, in former days, she had looked forward to the future with greater strength and different expectations, yet, even as it was, in spite of the cough and the painful pricking in her scars, she found it pleasant so long as she was free and could follow whatever way she chose. She knew the city, and limped through the streets and alleys toward the tavern where the strolling players usually lodged.

On the way she met a gentleman in a suit of light armour, whom she recognised in the distance as the Knight of Neckerfels, who had been paying court to her before her fall. He was walking alone and looked her directly in the face, but he did not have the slightest idea that he had met madcap Kuni. It was only too evident that he supposed her to be a total stranger. Yet it would have been impossible for any one to recognise her.

Mirrors were not allowed in the convent, but a bright new tin plate had showed her her emaciated face with the broad scar on the forehead, the sunken eyes, and the whole narrow head, where the hair, which grew out again very slowly, was just an ugly length. Now the sight of the bony hand which grasped the cane brought a half-sorrowful, half-scornful, smile to her lips. Her arm had been plump and round, but was now little larger than a stick. Pretty Kuni, the ropedancer, no longer existed; she must become accustomed to have the world regard her as a different and far less important personage, whom Lienhard, too—and this was fortunate — would not have deemed worthy of a glance.

And yet, if the inner self is the true one, there was little change in her. Her soul was moved by the same feelings, only there was now a touch of bitterness. One great advantage of her temperament, it is true, had vanished with her physical beauty and strength—the capacity to hope for happiness and joy. Perhaps it would never return; an oppressive feeling of guilt, usually foreign to her careless nature, had oppressed her ever since she had heard recently in the convent that the child on whom she had called down death and destruction was lying hopelessly ill, and would scarcely live till the joyous Whitsuntide.

This now came back to her mind. The jubilant sense of freedom deserted her; she walked thoughtfully on until she reached the neighbourhood of Jacob Fugger's house.

A long funeral procession was moving slowly toward her. Some very exalted and aristocratic person must be taking the journey to the grave, for it was headed by all the clergy in the city. Choristers, in the most elaborate dress, swinging incense holders by delicate metal chains and bearing lanterns on long poles, surrounded the lofty cross.

Every one of distinction in Augsburg, all the children who attended school, and all the members of the various ecclesiastical orders and guilds in the city marched before the bier. Kuni had never seen such a funeral procession. Perhaps the one she witnessed in Milan, when a great nobleman was buried, was longer, but in this every individual seemed to feel genuine grief. Even the schoolboys who, on such solemn occasions, usually play all sorts of secret pranks, walked as mournfully as if each had lost some relative who was specially dear to him. Among the girls there were few whose rosy cheeks were not constantly wet with tears.

From the first Kuni had believed that she knew who was being borne to the grave. Now she heard several women whispering near her mention the name of Juliane Peutinger. A pale-faced gold embroiderer, who had recently bordered a gala dress with leaves and tendrils for the dead girl's sister, described, sobbing, the severe suffering amid which this fairest blossom of Augsburg girlhood had withered ere death finally broke the slender stem.

Suddenly she stopped; a cry of mingled astonishment, lamentation, and delight, sometimes rising, sometimes falling, ran through the crowd which had gathered along the sides of the street.

The bier was in sight.

Twelve youths bore the framework, covered with a richly embroidered blue cloth, on which the coffin rested. It was open, and the dead girl's couch was so high that it seemed as though the sleeper was only resting lightly on the white silk pillow. A wreath again encircled her head, but this time blossoming myrtles blended with the laurel in the brown curls that lay in thick, soft locks on the snowy pillows and the lace- trimmed shroud.

Juliane's eyes were closed. Ah! how gladly Kuni would have kissed those long-lashed lids to win even one look of forgiveness from her whom her curse had perhaps snatched from the green spring world!

She remembered the sunny radiance with which this sleeper's eyes had sparkled as they met Lienhard's. They were the pure mirror of the keen, mobile intellect and the innocent, loving soul of this rare child. Now death had closed them, and Juliane's end had been one of suffering. The pale embroiderer had said so, and the sorrowful droop of the sweet little mouth, which gave the wondrously beautiful, delicate, touching little face so pathetic an expression, betrayed it. If the living girl had measured her own young intellect with that of grown people, and her face had worn the impress of precocious maturity, now it was that of a charming child who had died in suffering.

Kuni also felt this, and asked herself how it had been possible for her heart to cherish such fierce hatred against this little one, who had numbered only eleven years.

But had this Juliane resembled other children?

No, no! No Emperor's daughter of her age would have been accompanied to the churchyard with such pageantry, such deep, universal grief.

She had been the jewel of a great city. This was proclaimed by many a Greek and Latin maxim on tablets borne by the friends of the great humanist who, with joyful pride, called her his daughter.

Kuni could not read, but she heard at least one sentence translated by a Benedictine monk to the nun at his side: "He whose death compels those who knew him to weep, has the fairest end."—[Seneca, Hippol., 881.]

If this were true, Juliane's end was indeed fair; for she herself, whom the child had met only to inflict pain, had her eyes dimmed by tears, and wherever she turned she saw people weeping.

Most of those who lined the street could have had no close relations with the dead girl. But yonder black-robed mourners who followed the bier were her parents, her brothers and sisters, her nearest relatives, the members of the Council, and the family servants. And she, the wretched, reckless, sinful, crippled strolling player, for whom not a soul on earth cared, whose death would not have drawn even a single tear from any eye, to whom a speedy end could be only a benefit, was perhaps the cause of the premature drying up of this pure fountain of joy, which had refreshed so many hearts and animated them with the fairest hopes.

The tall lady, whose noble face and majestic figure were shrouded in a thick veil, was Juliane's mother—and she had offered the sick ropedancer a home in her wealthy household.

"If she had only known," thought Kuni, "the injury I was inflicting upon her heart's treasure, she would rather have hunted me with dogs from her threshold."

In spite of the veil which floated around the stately figure of the grieving mother, she could see her bosom rise and fall with her sobs of anguish. Kuni's compassionate heart made it impossible for her to watch this sorrow longer, and, covering her face with her hands, she turned her back upon the procession and, weeping aloud, limped away as fast as her injured foot would let her. Meanwhile she sometimes said to herself that she was the worst of all sinners because she had cursed the dead girl and called down death and destruction upon her head, sometimes she listened to the voice within, which told her that she had no reason to grieve over Juliane's death, and completely embitter her already wretched life by remorse and self-accusations; the dead girl was the sole cause of her terrible fall. But the defiant rebellion against the consciousness of guilt, which moved her so deeply, always ceased abruptly as soon as it raised its head; for one fact was positive, if the curse she had called down upon the innocent child, who had done her no intentional wrong, had really caused Juliane's end, a whole life was not long enough to atone for the sin which she had committed. Yet what atonement was still in her power, after the death which she had summoned had performed its terrible work of executioner?

"Nothing, nothing at all!" she said to herself angrily, resolving, as she had so often done with better success, to forget what had happened, cast the past into oblivion, and live in the present as before. But ere she could attempt to fulfil this determination, the image of the tall, grief- bowed figure of the woman who had called Juliane her dear child rose before her mind, and it seemed as if a cold, heavy hand paralyzed the wings of the light-hearted temperament which had formerly borne her pleasantly over so many things. Then she told herself that, in order not to go to perdition herself, she must vow, sacrifice, undertake everything for the salvation of the dead girl and of her own heavily burdened soul. For the first time she felt a longing to confide her feelings to some one. If Lienhard had been within reach and disposed to listen to her, he would have understood, and known what course to advise.

True, the thought that he was not looking at her when she took the fatal leap still haunted her. He could not have showed more offensively how little he cared for her—but perhaps he was under the influence of a spell; for she must be something to him. This was no vain self- deception; had it not been so, would he have come in person to her couch of pain, or cared for her so kindly after the accident?

In the convent she had reached the conviction that it would be degrading to think longer of the man who, in return for the most ardent love, offered nothing but alms in jingling coin; yet her poor heart would not cease its yearning.

Meanwhile she never wearied of seeking motives that would place his conduct in a more favourable light. Whatever he might have withheld from her, he was nevertheless the best and noblest of men, and as she limped aimlessly on, the conviction strengthened that the mere sight of him would dispel the mists which, on this sunny spring day, seemed to veil everything around and within her.

But he remained absent, and suddenly it seemed more disgraceful to seek him than to stand in the stocks.

Yet the pilgrimage to Compostella, of which the confessor had spoken? For the very reason that it had been described to her as unattainable, it would perhaps be rated at a high value in heaven, and restore to her while on earth the peace she had lost.

She pondered over this thought on her way to the tavern, where she found a corner to sleep, and a carrier who, on the day after the morrow, would take her to the sea for a heller pound. Other pilgrims had also engaged passage at Antwerp for Corunna, the harbour of Compostella, and her means were sufficient for the voyage. This assurance somewhat soothed her while she remained among people of her own calling.

But she spent a sleepless night; for again and again the dead child's image appeared vividly before her. Rising from the soft pillows in the coffin, she shook her finger threateningly at her, or, weeping and wailing, pointed down to the flames—doubtless those of purgatory—which were blazing upward around her, and had already caught the hem of her shroud.

Kuni arose soon after sunrise with a bewildered brain. Before setting out on her pilgrimage she wished to attend mass, and—that the Holy Virgin might be aware of her good intentions—repeat in church some of the paternosters which her confessor had imposed.

She went out with the simple rosary that the abbess had given her upon her wrist, but when she had left the tavern behind she saw a great crowd in front of the new St. Ulrich's Church, and recognised among the throngs of people who had flocked thither her companion in suffering at the convent, the keeper of the bath-house, who had been cured of her burns long before.

She had left her business to buy an indulgence for her own sins, and to purchase for the soul of her husband—whose death-bed confession, it is true, had been a long one—for the last time, but for many centuries at once, redemption from the fires of purgatory. The Dominican friar Tetzel, from Nuremberg, was here with his coffer, and carried written promises which secured certain remission of punishment for all sins, even those committed long ago, or to be committed in the future. The woman had experienced the power of his papers herself. Tetzel had come to Augsburg about a year after her husband's death, and, as she knew how many sins he had committed, she put her hand into her purse to free him from the flames. They must have burned very fiercely; for, while awake at night and in her dreams, she had often heard him wailing and complaining piteously. But after she bought the paper he became quiet and, on the third night, she saw him with her own eyes enter the room, and heard him promise her a great happiness in return for her faithful remembrance.

The very next Sunday, Veit Haselnuss, the bath-house proprietor, a well- to-do man who owned another house besides the one where he lived, invited her to take a walk with him. She knew instantly that her late husband was beginning to pay his debt of gratitude with this visitor and, in fact, a short time after, the worthy man asked her to be his wife, though she had three little children, and his oldest daughter by his first wife was already able to look after the housekeeping. The wedding took place on Whitsunday, and she owed this great happiness entirely to the dispensation which had released the dead man's soul from the fires of purgatory and induced him to show his thankfulness.

Kuni listened to her companion's rapid flood of talk, until she herself enjoined silence to hear the black-robed priest who stood beside the coffer.

He was just urging his hearers, in a loud voice, to abandon the base avarice which gathers pence. There was still time to gain, in exchange for dead florins, living salvation.

Let those who repented sin listen, and they would hear the voices of wailing parents, husbands, wives, brothers, sisters, and children, who had preceded them to the other world. Whose heart was so utterly turned to stone, whose parsimony, spite of all his love of money, was so strong that he would allow these tortured souls to burn and suffer in the flames, when it was in his power, by putting his hand into his purse, to buy a dispensation which would as surely redeem them from the fires of purgatory as his Imperial Majesty's pardon would release an imprisoned thief from jail?

Scales seemed to fall from Kuni's eyes. She hastily forced her way to the Dominican, who was just wiping the perspiration from his brow with the hem of the white robe under his black cowl.

Coughing and panting, he was preparing his voice for a fresh appeal, meanwhile opening the iron-bound box, and pointing out to the throng the placard beside his head, which announced that the money obtained by the indulgences was intended for the Turkish war. Then, in fluent language, he explained to the bystanders that this meant that the Holy Father in Rome intended to drive the hereditary foe of Christianity back to the steppes and deserts of the land of Asia, where he belonged. In order to accomplish this work, so pleasing to the Lord, the Church was ready to make lavish use of the treasures of mercy intrusted to her. Deliverance from the flames of purgatory would never be more cheaply purchased than at this opportunity. Then he thrust his little fat hand, on which several valuable rings glittered, into the box, and held out to the bystanders a small bundle of papers like an open pack of cards.

Kuni summoned up her courage and asked whether they would also possess the power to remove a curse. Tetzel eagerly assented, adding that he had papers which would wash the soul as white from every sin as soap would cleanse a sooty hand, even though, instead of "curse," its name was "parricide."

The most costly had the power to transfer scoundrels roasting in the hottest flames of purgatory to the joys of paradise, as yonder sparrow had just soared from the dust of the street to the elm bough.

Kuni timidly asked the price of an indulgence, but the Dominican unctuously explained that they were not sold like penny rolls at the baker's; the heavier the sin, the higher the fine to be paid. First of all, she must confess sincere contrition for what had been done and inform him how, in spite of her youth, she had been led into such heinous guilt. Kuni replied that she had long mourned her error most deeply, and then began to whisper to Tetzel how she had been induced to curse a fellow-mortal. She desired nothing for herself. Her sole wish was to release the dead girl from the flames of purgatory, and the curse which, by her guilt, burdened her soul. But the Dominican had only half listened, and as many who wanted indulgences were crowding around his box, he interrupted

Kuni by offering her a paper which he would make out in the name of the accursed Juliane Peutinger—if he had heard correctly.

Such cases seemed to be very familiar to him, but the price he asked was so large that the girl grew pale with terror.

Yet she must have the redeeming paper, and Tetzel lowered his price after her declaration that she possessed only five heller pounds and the convent viaticum. Besides, she stated that she had already bargained with the carrier for the journey to the sea.

This, however, had no influence upon the Dominican, as the indulgence made the pilgrimage to Compostella unnecessary. Since it would redeem the accursed person from the fires of purgatory, she, too, was absolved from the vow which drew her thither.

With stern decision he therefore insisted upon demanding the entire sum in her possession. He could only do it so cheaply because her face and her lost foot showed that she was destined to suffer part of the eternal torture here on earth.

Then Kuni yielded. The paper was made out in the name of Juliane, she gave up her little store, and returned to the inn a penniless beggar, but with a lighter heart, carrying the precious paper under the handkerchief crossed over her bosom. But there the carrier refused her a seat without the money which she had promised him, and the landlord demanded payment for her night's lodging and the bit of food she had eaten.

> Should she go back to the convent and ask for the little sum which Lienhard had left there for her?

The struggle was a hard one, but pride finally conquered. She renounced the kindly meant gift of her only friend. When the abbess returned the money to him, he could not help perceiving that she was no beggar and scorned to be his debtor. If he then asked himself why, he would find the right answer. She did not confess it to herself in plain words, but she wished to remain conscious that, whether he desired it or not, she had given her heart's best love to this one man without reward, merely because it was her pleasure to do it. At last she remembered that she still possessed something valuable. She had not thought of it before, because it had been as much a part of herself as her eyes or her lips, and it would have seemed utterly impossible to part with it. This article was a tolerably heavy gold ring, with a sparkling ruby in the centre. She had drawn it from her father's finger after he had taken his last leap and she was called to his corpse. She did not even know whether he had received the circlet as a wedding ring from the mother of whom she had no remembrance, or where he obtained it. But she had heard that it was of considerable value, and when she set off to sell the jewel, she did not find it very hard to gave it up. It seemed as if her father, from the grave, was providing his poor child with the means she needed to continue to support her life.

She had heard in the convent of Graslin, the goldsmith, who had bestowed on the chapel a silver shrine for the relics, and went to him.

When she stood before the handsome gableroofed house which he occupied she shrank back a little. At first he received her sternly and repellantly enough, but, as soon as she introduced herself as the ropedancer who had met with the accident, he showed himself to be a kindly old gentleman.

After one of the city soldiers had said that she told the truth and had just been dismissed from the convent, he paid her the full value of the ring and added a florin out of sympathy and the admiration he felt for the charm which still dwelt in her sparkling blue eyes.

But Compostella was indeed far away. Her new supply of money was sufficient for the journey there, but how could she return? Besides, her cough troubled her very seriously, and it seemed as though she could not travel that long distance alone. The dealer in indulgences had said that the paper made the pilgrimage unnecessary, and the confessor in the convent had only commanded her to go to Altotting. With this neighbouring goal before her, she turned her back upon Augsburg the following morning.

Her hope of meeting on the way compassionate people, who would give her a seat in their vehicles, was fulfilled. She reached Altotting sooner than she had expected. During the journey, sometimes in a peasant's cart, sometimes in a freight wagon, she had thought often of little Juliane, and always with a quiet, nay, a contented heart. In the famous old church, at the end of her pilgrimage, she saw a picture in which the raked souls of children were soaring upward to heaven from the flames blazing around them in purgatory.

The confessor had sent her to the right place.

Here a fervent prayer had the power to rescue a child's soul from the fires of purgatory. Many other votive pictures, the pilgrims at the inn, and a priest whom she questioned, confirmed it. She also heard from various quarters that she had not paid too high a price for the indulgence. This strengthened her courage and henceforward, nay, even during the time of sore privation which she afterward endured, she blessed a thousand times her resolve to buy the ransoming paper from Tetzel, the Dominican; for she thought that she daily experienced its power.

Whenever Juliane appeared, her face wore a friendly expression—nay, once, in a dream, she floated before her as if she wished to thank her, in the form of a beautiful angel with large pink and white wings. She no longer needed to fear the horrible curse which she had called down upon the little one, and once more thought of Lienhard with pleasure. When he learned in the other world how she had atoned for the wrong which she had done his little favourite, she would be sure of his praise.

To be held in light esteem, nay, even despised, was part of her calling, like her constant wandering. She had longed for applause in her art, but for herself she had desired nothing save swift draughts of pleasure, since she had learned how little she was regarded by the only person whose opinion she valued. She could never have expected that he would hold her in high esteem, since he was so indifferent to her art that he did not even think it worth while to lift his eyes to the rope. Yet the idea that he placed her in the same rank with others in her profession seemed unendurable. But she need grieve over this no longer, and when she remembered that even the sorest want had not been able to induce her to touch his alms, she could have fairly shouted for joy amid all her misery. The conviction that one man, who was the best and noblest of his sex, might deem her a poor, unfortunate girl, but never a creature who deserved contempt, was the beam to which she clung, when the surges of her pitiable, wandering life threatened to close over her and stifle her.